PTEROSAUR TOMATO
AND
THE VILLAGE STORM

JANE MARRINER

AuthorHouse™ UK
1663 Liberty Drive
Bloomington, IN 47403 USA
www.authorhouse.co.uk
UK TFN: 0800 0148641 (Toll Free inside the UK)
UK Local: 02036 956322 (+44 20 3695 6322 from outside the UK)

Because of the dynamic nature of the Internet, any web addresses or links contained in
this book may have changed since publication and may no longer be valid. The views
expressed in this work are solely those of the author and do not necessarily reflect the
views of the publisher, and the publisher hereby disclaims any responsibility for them.

This book is printed on acid-free paper.

ISBN: 979-8-8230-8276-1 (sc)
ISBN: 979-8-8230-8277-8 (e)

Library of Congress Control Number: 2023909667

Print information available on the last page.

Published by AuthorHouse 05/25/2023

author HOUSE®

PTEROSAURR TOMATO
AND
THE VILLAGE STORM

Cordelia Corncob lived by the main road running through the village. She shared her house with Dango Dog who wore a different decorated collar every day of the week.

Farmer Fred owned the field next to Cordelia Corncob's house, and he had a pet cow called Clarissa.

The weather had been very hot of late, and Farmer Fred had used his combine harvester to bring in all the golden grain from his field. He invited Cordelia Corncob to pick up the remaining straw, which she placed in a basket always carried around on her head.

Cordelia Corncob made the straw into corn dollies which she gave to all the village children, and to whoever particularly liked them.

Cordelia Corncob's niece, Nesta, once gave her a present of a picture she had painted. This picture took pride of place in Cordelia Corncob's hallway. It was of a Pterosaur, which was a prehistoric flying reptile with a long neck, a huge wing span, long legs, and sporting a jaunty crest on whis head. Niece Nesta had depicted him with a beautiful tomato red jacket adorned with flowers. Of course, Cordelia Corncob had named him "Tomato".

Soon, the sun disappeared behind the clouds, and a fierce storm raged over the village. There was deafening thunder, forked lightning and torrential rain which swept down the main road, flooding all the nearby houses.

Bob the Boat had a motorboat in his garage which he often took to the seaside on his trailer, to give the village children a day out sailing. Now, he pulled the motorboat out of the garage into the swirling, whirling water. Bob the Boat rescued those whose houses were flooded.

There was Hannah McCluck with her three hens, and George and Georgina with Baby Bo. Also clambering aboard the boat came Bettina Bird with her talking budgerigar, and Sophie Sweet with a huge tin of fudge. There was Molly Mog who was missing her Cat Skittles. He had been frightened away by the thunder and had disappeared.

"We must get to the village hall, away from the floods, and we shall be safe there," decided Bob the Boat.

Meanwhile, Farmer Fred and Clarissa Cow stomped into Cordelia Corncob's house in their wellingtons, to offer their help.

"Thank goodness, all the grain was harvested before this terrible storm. The drains in the road are too small to take all the rushing water, and the whole old village draining system needs updating." Thus spoke Farmer Fred who knew about such things.

Suddenly, a flash of forked lightning struck Cordelia Corncob's house, severing the roof in half, and causing damage all the way to the ground. They all leapt sideways, and Niece Nesta's painting fell on the floor. Out stepped Pterosaur Tomato. He huffed and puffed until he was almost the size of the house.

"That's better, free at last!", Pterosaur Tomato declared happily. "Now, how can I be of assistance?"

Once, over the shock, Farmer Fred asked timidly if Pterosaur Tomato could kindly fly them all to the village hall to join everyone else.

"Gladly" replied Pterosaur Tomato, straightening his beautiful red jacket which had creased up in the lightning strike."Just jump on my back and we will fly through the gap in the roof."

Dango Dog and Clarissa Cow weren't so sure about it all, but were reassured by the others, and anyway, didn't want to be left behind. Pterosaur Tomato spread his wings and they flew into the sky and towards the village hall.

Clarissa Cow spied Little Billy Boy clinging to a branch at the top of a tree, which was standing in water. Pterosaur Tomato hovered near, and Cordelia Corncob held up her basket for Little Billy Boy to fall inside.

"Thank you, thank you" cried Little Billy Boy as he snuggled up to Dango Dog. Farmer Fred reached for his mobile 'phone to assure Little Billy Boy's parents that he was safe and well.

Further down, they saw Cat Skittles floundering in the water.

"I can't swim!" she meowed. "Please help me."

Dango Dog took off his dog collar and Cordelia Corncob threaded a string of corn dollies through the buckle to lengthen it. Then, they all shouted "CATCH!" Cat Skittles was heaved out of the water and onto Pterosaur Tomato's back. She was able to wave to Molly Mog who was leaning out of the boat below. Molly Mog clapped her hands in delight, and called out her thanks for Cat Skittle's rescue

When they all reached the village hall, they met with those whose homes had not been flooded or damaged, but had come to exchange greetings and to offer help.

Molly Mog went into the village hall kitchen and prepared egg dishes from Hannah McCluck's hens, and milk drinks courtesy of Clarissa Cow. Sophie Sweet handed round her delicious home made fudge.

Betsy Button settled down to sew buttons onto her new scarf. She always covered her new clothes with buttons from her pretty button box.

Conrad the Conjuror wanted to try out his conjuring tricks. He asked for a vwolunteer for an item to use in one of his tricks. Betsy Button offered her new scarf which he pushed up his sleeve but promptly lost it, much to everyone's disappointment. Dango Dog and Cat Skittles then found it on the floor behind Conrad the Conjuror.

"My dog collar is hanging up to dry, this scarf would be lovely to wear" said Dango Dog, wistfully as he handed it back to Betsy Button.

"Thank you, Dango Dog, but you keep it, it will suit you wonderfully," she said.

George and Georgina sat next to Bettina Bird. Her talking budgerigar recited a nursery rhyme making Baby Bo giggle and gurgle.

Melvin Melody had brought his violin, and he entertained everybody by playing well known tunes, which were much appreciated.

Little Billy Boy then sang something from the "chart topper", and was accompanied by Farmer Fred. He sat astride Clarissa Cow while beating out the rhythm with a spoon and saucepan from the kitchen.

"Encore, encore!" demanded them all.

All the while, Cordelia Corncob had been creating her corn dollies from the straw in her basket, and she gave everybody one as a keepsake.

Pterosaur Tomato told stories of prehistoric times, and was given grateful thanks for all his help.

Eventually, the storm passed over the village, and the sun smiled down again.

Bob the Boat revved up the motorboat and took his passengers back to their homes.

The storm damage was repaired with a lot of hard work, and together, everyone managed to fix Cordelia Corncob's roof.

Pterosaur Tomato was anxious to fly off to give aid elsewhere. Cordelia Corncob gave him two corn dollies, one of herself, and one of Dango Dog so that he wouldn't forget them, and the day's adventure..

Cordelia Corncob hugged him, and she and Dango Dog bid him good luck, and a fond farewell.

Pterosaur Tomato promised that he would come back to visit in the not too distant future.

Next day, the village was no longer waterlogged. The residents met to recount everything, and they all breathed a sigh of relief that no one had come to any harm. They happily resumed their daily lives again, but would never forget the storm of storms, and of course, meeting delightful Pterosaur Tomato.

Printed in the United States
by Baker & Taylor Publisher Services